Once upon a time, there was a rich sultan, who lived in a huge palace with hundreds of rooms. The palace was surrounded by fantastic gardens with trees, flowers, and fountains. The Sultan also had a huge stable where he kept lots of animals. All of the animals were well cared for and well fed.

The Sultan's favorite animal was a huge elephant. He had been given the elephant as a gift. Because the Sultan loved the elephant, he had his own roomy stall to live in, plenty of food, and even his own servant.

However, despite all of this, the elephant often felt lonely.

His stall had a window, but the window had bars across it to stop anyone getting into the palace. The elephant would look out of the window and across the city square. He could see the hustle and bustle of the market.

However, life outside the Sultan's palace wasn't always happy. Just outside the palace lived a stray dog. The dog was dirty and thin, as he had no one to care for him. He could smell the elephant's food and he would listen as the keeper talked to the elephant and brushed him.

One day the dog noticed that the palace gates had been left open. The guards were looking at two men arguing on the other side of the square. The dog slipped into the palace. Carefully, he made his way to the elephant's stable.

The dog hid in the corner of the stall, and because he was very thin no one noticed him. It was dry in the stable, with soft straw to sleep on, and he would eat the rice that the elephant dropped. As time went on, the elephant became aware that he shared his stall and food with a dog.

At first, the elephant was angry.

"What do you think you are doing?" trumpeted the elephant.

The dog explained that he had no one to care for him, and that he had been so very hungry. The kind elephant let him stay and, as time went on, the elephant and the dog became firm friends.

The elephant was not the only one to notice the dog. The elephant's keeper also saw him, but as the dog didn't do any harm, the keeper didn't say anything. The dog took to going with the elephant whenever he went out, trotting along underneath the elephant's belly so that the Sultan didn't see him.

A rich merchant, visiting the city, also saw the dog. By now the dog was sleek, with shiny fur, and a long wagging tail. The merchant spoke to the elephant keeper and offered him lots of cash for the dog. The keeper took the cash and gave the dog to the merchant.

The elephant could not understand where his friend had gone. He was very sad, and stopped eating and drinking. He didn't want to shower or be brushed, so he became very smelly. All day he would just stare out of his window looking for his dog friend.

When the Sultan came to visit his elephant he was very concerned.

"What has happened to my lovely elephant?" he wailed. "He was always so big and happy, and now he just stands there and smells."

The Sultan told his first minister to find out what was the matter.

The first minister went to the keeper and demanded to know what was wrong with the elephant. At first, the keeper said that he didn't know, but after a while he told them that he had sold the elephant's friend, the dog. He shook as he admitted that he didn't know where the dog was now.

When the Sultan had listened to the sad tale, he declared that the dog must be found and returned. Messengers were sent out to find the merchant. If the merchant would not return the dog, the Sultan threatened to punish him harshly.

After a while, the messengers reached the village where the merchant lived. He heard what the Sultan had threatened and became frightened that he would be punished. He chased the dog out of his yard and away down the road. The dog was very sad to be out on the streets again.

When the dog got to the village square, he stopped and was amazed to see the messenger and the elephant keeper.

He ran up to the keeper, jumping up and down, and barking, “It’s me! It’s me! I’m here!”

The keeper recognized the dog, and they returned happily to the Sultan and the elephant.

The elephant and the dog were overjoyed to be together again. The elephant wrapped his trunk around the dog and hugged him. Because the elephant was happy again, he started eating, and allowed his keeper to shower and brush him again. Nobody ever tried to part the friends again and they lived together happily ever after.